The Adventure of
the Strange Ruby

They heard nothing more for a whole week, and then another letter turned up – a rather grubby, creased one, which held only a few lines.

Only have a moment to scribble this – we're going off somewhere now, this minute, in a car. Things aren't too good, somehow. All we know is that we overheard someone mention Bringking Hill – at least that's what it *sounded* like. We're throwing this letter out of the car hoping it will be found and posted by someone. We'll write again if we can.

Faith

Other Enid Blyton titles available in Beaver

Adventure of the Strange Ruby

Enid Blyton

Illustrated by David Barnett

Beaver Books

A Beaver Book
Published by Arrow Books Limited
62–65 Chandos Place, London WC2N 4NW

An imprint of Century Hutchinson Limited

London Melbourne Sydney Auckland
Johannesburg and agencies throughout the world

First published by Hodder and Stoughton Children's Books 1960
Beaver edition 1979
Reprinted 1980, 1983, 1984 (twice) and 1988

Set in Baskerville

Printed and bound in Great Britain by
Cox & Wyman Ltd, Reading

ISBN 0 09 958230 9

Contents

1 A little bit of news

It all began when Pat picked up the paper one morning and read a little paragraph tucked away in a corner.

He was first down for breakfast. Not even his father was down yet, so Pat was able to have a look at the paper first. That didn't often happen.

The headlines weren't interesting – something about wage freezes, whatever that meant. Pat's eyes slid down the page and came to four small paragraphs. They were headed The Strange Ruby.

He read the paragraphs and then read them again. He was just finishing when he heard footsteps coming down the stairs, and his sister Tessa burst into the room.

'Goodness – I thought I was late,' she said in relief. 'Aren't Mummy and Daddy down yet?'

'No. I bet Daddy's lost his stud again,' said Pat. 'I've heard a lot of scrambling going on upstairs. I say, Tessa – look here – at this piece in the paper.'

Tessa took the paper and read the paragraphs out loud.

THE STRANGE RUBY

This sinister ruby, the biggest in the world, is once more in the news. For centuries it gleamed in the forehead of a great idol in a temple on an Indian hillside, one of a pair of enormous ruby eyes.

During a tribal war both rubies were stolen. One has never been found. The other eventually found its way into the hands of a powerful Indian ruler, who, in return for the saving of his life, gave it to an Englishman, Major Ellis Gathergood.

He died suddenly and the ruby passed to another member of the family. But misfortune has continually followed the owners of the ruby, and one member of the Gathergood family let it be known that he had sold the strange ruby. It has certainly never been heard of to this day.

It was, however, always believed to be in the possession of Mrs Eleanor Gathergood, who has just died. If so, the sinister ruby will pass to her nearest relatives, twins of 12, Faith and David Gathergood. What will they do with it?

Tessa read the paragraphs and looked up in excitement at Pat.

'Why – they must be the twins we met down at Swanage last year! They were good sports, weren't they?'

'Yes. They had a governess, do you remember?' said Pat. 'We were sorry for them because they hadn't any parents – only a great-aunt or someone like that.'

'And she must be the Mrs Eleanor Gathergood who has just died,' said Tessa. 'I say – have you kept the twins' address, Pat? Let's write and ask them if they really do own the strange ruby. They might show it to us.'

'I bet they wouldn't be allowed to have it on show,' said Pat, scornfully. 'But it wouldn't be a bad idea to write.'

'It says "Misfortune has continually followed the owners of the ruby",' said Tessa, looking at the paper again. 'I hope bad luck doesn't come to David and Faith – they've had quite enough already.'

'Yes – having your mother and father killed in a car accident is enough bad luck to last you for the rest of your life,' said Pat. 'Hallo – here's Dad at last.'

Their father came into the room and looked surprised to see Tessa and Pat down first.

'Turning over a new leaf?' he asked and

picked up the paper. 'Mother's just coming. Didn't you know the hall clock was fast?'

'Goodness, no,' said Pat. 'I simply *leapt* out of bed when I heard it strike eight. I bet you put it fast on purpose, Dad, because we were so late yesterday.'

'I wouldn't be surprised,' said his mother, coming in and sitting down behind the teapot. 'Well – any news in the paper?'

Pat told her about the piece he had read, and she nodded. 'Yes – those must be the twins we met last year. And now I come to think of it, their governess said she was upset because their great-aunt was ill, and she was afraid that, if she died, that strange ruby might be left to the twins. And I remember I was disgusted to hear her say that if it did, she would leave them at once, because she was afraid *she* might share in any bad luck that came to them through the old ruby.'

'What nonsense!' said her husband.

'I liked those twins,' said Tessa. 'I'm sure we still have their home address somewhere. We're going to write and ask them if they own the ruby now, Mummy.'

'They probably won't be told,' said her mother, pouring out the tea. 'I was sorry for those children – they seemed so completely on their own – no parents, no aunts or uncles or cousins. I was glad you made friends with them.'

11

After breakfast Pat and Tessa went up to their playroom and rummaged about in their desks. As usual they were in a terrible muddle. It was a wonder they ever found anything they wanted.

Tessa at last found the address she was looking for. She pulled out an old notebook and flourished it.

'Here's my address book – haven't seen it since last year. Now I'll look for the twins' address.'

She flipped over the pages and then came to a stop. 'Here it is – David and Faith, Hailey House, Tipscombe, Wilts. Let's write today.'

'All right – you do the letter,' said Pat, who never wrote to anyone if he could help it.

So Tessa wrote the letter – and that was how it was that she and Pat came to share in the extraordinary adventure of the Strange Ruby.

2 Two interesting letters

No answer came to Tessa's letter for some time. 'I expect it had to be forwarded from their home address to their school,' said Tessa. 'They go to boarding-school, don't they, not to day-school, like us.'

The end of term came, and still there was no answer. Then, on the third day of the summer holidays, there came a letter addressed to Tessa. It was from Faith.

'Now we'll hear their news,' said Tessa, tearing open the envelope. Pat came and looked over her shoulder. They read in silence.

Dear Tessa and Pat,

Thanks awfully for your letter. Yes, it was our great-aunt who died. We were rich before, and now I suppose we're richer which is an awful nuisance, because what we really want to do when we're older is just to run a riding-stables, and you don't want a lot of money for that.

At least, if you do, you can earn it, and that's fun. Just having money left to you is no fun at all. AND we've got the Ruby — at least, it's being kept for us, though goodness knows we don't want the beastly thing. We haven't seen it.

Do you remember our governess, Miss Lawley? Well, she's gone. She's afraid of the Ruby! Can you imagine anything so idiotic — afraid of a red stone! She told us awful things about it before she went, tried to scare us, but you know David and me, we laughed like anything at her.

We're having someone else soon, I don't know who. Someone mouldy, I expect — couldn't be worse than old Lawley, anyway, with her scare-stories!

We're going somewhere for the hols. I don't know where, because for some reason or other it's all hush-hush. If only it was Swanage again! If we can manage to find out where we're going, we'll send a note. David sends you one of his grins.

Love from
Faith Gathergood

Tessa looked at Pat. 'So their governess kept her word! Well, she couldn't have been very fond of them. It must be pretty awful to have nobody fond of you, no mother or anything.'

'Well, they've got each other, and you know what twins are,' said Pat. 'They stick together like glue, usually. I do hope they'll manage to let us know where they're going for the hols. I only wish it was somewhere near us.'

They heard nothing more for a whole week, and then another letter turned up – rather a grubby, creased one, which held only a few lines.

Only have a moment to scribble this – we're going off somewhere now, this minute, in a car. Things aren't too good, somehow. All we know is that we overheard someone mention Bringking Hill – at least that's what it sounded like. We're throwing this letter out of the car hoping it will be found and posted by someone. We'll write again if we can.

Faith

Pat and Tessa read this twice. Then they looked at one another.

'What does Faith mean – "things aren't too good, somehow", do you suppose?' said Pat. 'And why weren't they told where they were going? They must have asked! And why on earth weren't they allowed even to post a letter?'

'It seems a bit funny,' said Tessa. 'But, of

course, the twins always were a bit mad, and given to making mysteries out of things, weren't they? We'll probably get a letter or card in a day or two with their proper address.'

But they didn't. No letter or card came at all. Then, for some reason, Tessa began to worry.

'I'm sure there's something up,' she said. 'I've got one of my Feelings. I think we ought to tell Mummy.'

'Don't be so silly,' said Pat. 'You and your Feelings! The last time you had a Feeling, it was about Dumpy the cat, and you gave me an awful time, making me think she had been run over and killed or something – and she was in the kitchen all the time.'

'But she had stolen all the fish out of the larder,' said Tessa.

'Oh well – if you're going to have Feelings about cats stealing fish, I don't think much of them,' said Pat. 'But I'll tell you what we'll do, Tessa – we'll look up Daddy's hotel and garage book, that gives all the towns of Britain, and see if Bringking Hill is mentioned.'

There was no mention of Bringking Hill, but there was apparently a town called Brinkin – and what was more, it was in Dorset, not so very far from Swanage, which the children knew very well indeed!

'Gosh – suppose this Brinkin is the Bringking Hill Faith writes about!' said Pat. 'We're going down to Dorset soon – we might be able to find Brinkin Hill, if it's near Brinkin, and see if we can spot the twins!'

'Let's get the big map of Dorset,' said Tessa. 'Where is it? Oh, I know – it's in the cupboard with all the other maps. I'll get it.'

She found it, and the two of them spread out the big, detailed map on the playroom floor and studied it very carefully.

Pat spotted Brinkin first and jabbed his finger on it triumphantly.

'There you are – Brinkin – and look at this nearby, it's a hill. I bet it's Brinkin Hill!'

'It's not *terribly* far from Swanage,' said Tessa considering the map. 'We'd have to go through Corfe Castle village – and take this road here.'

'Well – as soon as we get down to Swanage this year, let's cycle to Brinkin Hill and find the twins!' cried Pat. 'What a surprise we'll give them!'

3 Off to find Brinkin Hill

At last the day came when the two children were to go off to Swanage.

'Four whole weeks!' said Pat in delight. 'We'll bathe and ride and sail – and, of course, we'll go to Brinkin Hill. If only it's the same place that the twins meant in their letter!'

Swanage was just the same as ever – a great wide bay of forget-me-not blue, with hardly a ripple or a wave, except just at the edge. Behind rose the glorious hills. The sun shone warmly, and the very first thing that Pat and Tessa did, of course, was to fling off their clothes, put on bathing things and prance into the water.

'Ooooh – it's cold after all,' said Tessa in surprise. 'And it looked so warm!'

'This is the very first day of the very first week,' said Pat, splashing Tessa, 'and the first days will go beautifully slowly. Then they'll glide away at top speed without being noticed. But oh, how gorgeous the very beginning is.'

'Yes – with heaps of days in front of you,' said Tessa, who was in the water properly now and swimming beside Pat. 'I say – this patch of water is lovely and warm. I'm going to turn over and float in it.'

For the first four days Tessa and Pat hardly thought of the twins at all. There were so many lovely things to do. Then Tessa spoke about them.

'We've forgotten Faith and David. What about cycling over to Brinkin to see if we can find the hill, and any house there that the twins might be living in. The post-office might know.'

'Yes. We'll go over today,' said Pat. 'Mother will give us sandwiches.'

So at half past ten they set off on their bicycles, each with a basket packed full of neat parcels of food.

'You can buy yourselves drinks,' their mother said. 'And I have no doubt you will fill yourselves up with ice-creams, too. I'll expect you back when I see you. Have a good day!'

The two cycled off. They took the Corfe Castle direction and marvelled, as always, when they came to the ancient little village, dominated by the centuries-old ruined castle, dreaming by itself high upon the hill.

'There's such a lovely *old* feeling here,' said Tessa as they cycled round the hill on which the castle stood. The jackdaws wheeled above it, calling chack-chack-chack in their loud, cheerful voices. 'Gosh, isn't it hot, Pat? I could do with an ice-cream and a drink already, couldn't you?'

'Let's get just a *bit* thirstier and hotter, then we'll enjoy them all the more,' said Pat. So on they went, panting in the hot sun, though they really had very little on.

A lane led off the main road to Brinkin. It wasn't a town, after all, but a big village. It lay in a little hollow surrounded by trees, and a farm or two spread out on each side. Behind was a very steep hill, closely wooded.

'I should think that *must* be Brinkin Hill,' said Pat. 'Let's find a shop that sells ice-creams and ask.'

They soon found a shop. It was a typical little village shop, half post-office and half everything else. It seemed to sell potatoes as well as stamps, lemonade and ice-cream, as well as postal orders, sun-hats, socks, rope, kettles, saucepans, chocolate and goodness knows what besides.

'This is the kind of shop I like,' said Pat, looking round. 'If I kept a shop I should keep one just like this.'

'Yes – and keep it all muddly, too,' said Tessa. 'I can just see your shop, Pat – you'd never be able to find a thing!'

They sat on a little seat outside, drank their lemonade out of the bottles, and scraped the ice-cream out of its cartons.

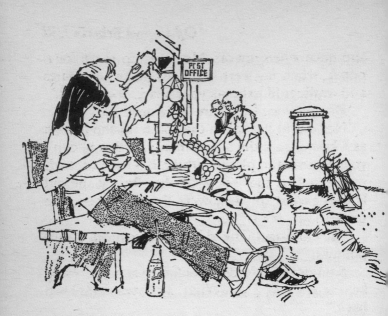

'Delicious!' said Tessa. 'I hope the man who invented ice-cream had medals hung all over him!'

They took the bottles back and spoke to the old lady behind the post-office counter.

'Could you tell us if that is Brinkin Hill over there?'

'You're right,' said the old woman in her pleasant Dorset voice. 'That be Brinkin Hill – but don't you be going there. It's too steep.'

'Does anyone live up on the hill?' asked Tessa.

'Well, there's an old house there, Brinkin Towers,' said the woman. 'Been shut up for years, it has – yes, and no one durst go near it, for 'tis said there were queer goings-on there once;

and once when my old Ma went up there for a prank, when she were a girl, she heard weepings and wailings fit to break your heart. So she said.'

'Does anyone live there now?' said Pat.

'Not a soul has taken that path up the hill far as I know,' said the old woman. 'I tell you, don't you go near the place – it's bad. There's a high wall round it too - you can hardly see the old house, except for its towers showing above the trees.'

The children thanked her and went off, disappointed.

'Sounds as if it's most unlikely the twins would be there,' said Pat. 'What shall we do? Turn back?'

'No,' said Tessa, suddenly. 'I want to go on. I want to see what Brinkin Towers is like. Come on – there's no harm in trying.'

4 Up to Brinkin Towers

The children mounted their bicycles and rode off in the direction of the hill. They came to a steep road that led upwards. It was merely a narrow lane, and as the hedges had not been clipped for years, hawthorn and other trees almost touched overhead!

Pat jumped off his bicycle and so did Tessa. It was impossible to ride up such a steep lane. It was a very stony road, too, and they didn't want to get punctures from the flints that lay about.

The lane grew narrower as it went up, and soon became overgrown with weeds and grass.

'No car could possibly come up here with the lane in this condition, Tessa,' said Pat. 'And see here – there's a bramble right across the road, from one side of the hedge to the other. It really does look as if nobody's been this way for years. Let's go back.'

'All right – go back then,' said Tessa, beginning to feel hot and cross, but also obstinate.

24

'I'm going on by myself. Just like you to give up.'

'It is not,' said Pat, pushing on at once. 'If you're going on, then so am I. Though goodness knows what for.'

They went on in silence, except for puffs and pants. Little streams of perspiration ran down their faces, and they began to long for another ice-cream and a drink. No, two ice-creams and two drinks! Perhaps even three.

The lane curved suddenly, and then came to a complete stop outside a great wooden gate that was crossed and recrossed with iron bars in a strange pattern. The two children stood in front of it, staring up. The top was set with wicked-looking iron spikes.

'Gosh – look at that! It might be the gate of some castle,' said Pat. He went up to it and pushed at it. It did not budge in the least, of course, but stood there, stolid and immovable.

'Bolted at the back, I suppose,' said Pat. 'Look, there's a piece of ivy that has grown from the wall half across the gate!'

'Yes – and that definitely proves that no one has opened this gate for ages,' said Tessa, at once. 'Or the ivy would have been wrenched off when the gate opened. No one can possibly live here now, that's certain.'

'What a frightfully high wall goes all round it,' said Pat. 'And set with those awful spikes too. They certainly meant to keep people out. If there *were* queer-goings-on here, as that old woman said, the owners didn't mean anyone to see them!'

'Let's walk round the wall and see how far it goes,' said Tessa, putting her bicycle against a tree. 'We'll go all the way round and back again to this gate. That's if we can make our way all right!'

'You do think of mad ideas,' groaned Pat, but as he couldn't bear Tessa to do anything without him, he put his bicycle down too, and followed her.

It was certainly very difficult in places to make their way round the wall. Bushes and trees grew right up to it, and the undergrowth was so thick that the two children had almost to force their way through it.

'I call this a mad idea,' said Pat again. 'I vote we go back.'

'Well, that's silly – we must be more than half-way round already!' said Tessa. 'It will be quicker to get back to the gate if we go *on* – not if we go back!'

Pat followed Tessa. When they were about half-way round she stopped with a sudden exclamation. They had come out on to a clear piece of hillside. They looked down, not on Brinkin Village, which was now on the other side of the hill, of course, but on a curious little lake, set thickly round with trees. The water shone blue as the

sky. Not far from the shore of the secret lake was a small island full of trees. In the midst of the trees was a little building with queer pointed towers.

'Look at that!' said Tessa, suddenly speaking in a whisper, though she couldn't think why. 'A lake! It wasn't marked on the map, was it?'

'Too small, perhaps,' said Pat. 'And too secret! Why, nobody except the people who lived here would be able to see that lake, I should think. I wonder what that funny little building is on the island – it looks very odd, somehow.'

'I expect it's a summer-house or boat-house or something,' said Tessa. 'What a wonderful view! I wonder how the people got down to the lake from Brinkin Towers, Pat. The lake must have belonged to the house – how did they reach it?'

'There must be a way down,' said Pat. Then he looked at Tessa, suddenly struck by a bright idea. 'And what's more there must be a door set in this side of the wall, so that the people who lived here could walk down from the grounds to the lake. They wouldn't go out of that big front gate and walk all the way round the walls, as we have.'

'Let's look for a door in the wall then, shall we?' said Tessa, excited.

They walked on round the thick, high wall for some way – and then Tessa gave a sudden exclamation.

'Pat! Here it is – a little door set deep in the wall. Look!'

Sure enough there was a door – and leading up to it was a path. The children stared at it in silence. Then Pat spoke.

'Someone's used this path lately. It's all trampled, look. Someone's been in through this door – and nobody knows about them. Who are they, Tessa? That's what I'd like to know!'

5 Inside the walls

Tessa went to the door in the thick wall and pushed at it. She turned the looped iron handle, but the door would not open.

'Locked on the other side, Tessa,' said Pat, in a low voice. 'Whoever has come here has come secretly, and you may be sure every door will be well and truly locked. But isn't it queer?'

'Yes,' said Tessa, puzzled. 'Pat – you don't think the twins could possibly be *here*, do you?'

'I shouldn't think so,' said Pat. 'I can't see why anyone should come for a holiday in this peculiar place. Anyway – I dare say there's some explanation of the trampled path. Maybe someone comes in each day and dusts the house or something.'

'Where from?' demanded Tessa at once. 'If it was anyone from the village it would be known – and there doesn't seem to be a single cottage nearby.'

'I suppose we can't possibly get into the

grounds, can we?' said Pat, after a pause. 'I mean – if there's any chance of the twins being here – which, of course, I don't really believe – we ought to try and see them and find out what's happening. Their last letter sounded a bit worried.'

'That's all very well – but how do you think we're going to climb over a 10-feet-high wall with those awful spikes at the top?' said Tessa, scornfully. 'I don't want to be jabbed to pieces, if you do!'

An overgrown path cut with steps led down to the secret lake. The children didn't think they would go down. Somehow they felt safer up by the wall.

'Let's go on round the wall,' said Tessa, at last. 'It's about the only thing left to do.'

So they went on again, pushing their way through the undergrowth – and then suddenly Pat clutched at Tessa and stopped her. He pointed silently upwards.

She looked up to the top of the wall. A tree had fallen against it just there and had broken off the top layer of bricks with its ugly spikes. There was a gap – without spikes!

'We could shin up the tree and see over the wall from the top there, where it's broken,' whispered Pat.

Tessa nodded. An excited feeling welled up in her, and she felt suddenly out of breath. She watched Pat climb carefully up the tree that leaned against the wall, and then he sat on the top, where it was broken. Tessa followed him, tearing her jeans against a sharp twig, but not even noticing it.

There was not room for both children at the top of the wall, for the broken gap was not very large. Tessa peeped over Pat's shoulder.

They saw a great house with towers at each end. They could see little of the lower part of the building because high trees surrounded it. They gazed at the big dark windows. Most of them had thick curtains pulled right across.

But one window, up on the second floor, had no curtains pulled across – and, as Pat and Tessa watched, they saw a movement behind the window. Then a face looked out – but what kind of face they were too far away to see.

Tessa clutched Pat and made him jump so much that he nearly fell off the wall.

'Don't,' he whispered, fiercely. 'What's up? Did *you* see someone at the window, too?'

'Yes. Who is it?' whispered Tessa. 'Oh, Pat – suppose it's the twins – and they're locked up here! Nobody would ever know. They've got no parents or relations.'

'It probably isn't the twins,' said Pat, gruffly. 'But all the same – we'll try and find out. There's certainly something peculiar about all this. People coming secretly to this deserted old house; coming to that door in the wall instead of through the village, up the lane and in at the front gate. Who are they, anyway?'

'Shall we swing ourselves on to the branch of that tree nearby that grows on the inner side of the wall?' said Tessa. 'It looks easy to climb down.'

'Right. But don't miss getting hold of the branch,' said Pat. 'I'll go first. And mind – if anyone meets us, we're just exploring, see? Don't say a word about the twins.'

Soon they were both over the wall and down on the ground. The undergrowth was as thick here as on the other side of the wall – even thicker, it seemed to Tessa, whose legs were getting very scratched indeed. So were Pat's, but he didn't seem to mind.

They made their way cautiously towards the house, hiding behind trees whenever they trod on a twig that cracked, in case anyone had heard it. But there seemed to be nobody about at all.

They stood at last behind a bush from which they could see the second-floor window that had no curtains drawn across it. They both peered up. No face was at the window now.

'What shall we do next?' whispered Pat. 'I daren't go to find a door – we'd have to pass windows on the ground floor, and if they had their curtains drawn back, we might be seen.'

'Couldn't we throw a stone up to that second-floor window?' whispered Tessa. 'If there's someone there, they would hear the noise of the stone and come to the window. Then we might be able to see if it was the twins or not.'

'Right – I'll throw one,' said Pat. He found two or three small stones and threw one up. It hit the wall just under the window. He tried again – and his aim was not only good, but much too hard!

CRASH! The window broke. What a tremendous noise it seemed to make in those still grounds! Pat and Tessa squeezed under the thick bush immediately. *Now* what would happen?

6 A great surprise

Under the bush the two children began to tremble with excitement and sudden fear. Pat hadn't meant to break the window. What a dreadful thing to do! Ought he to go and own up?

Above them, from the second-floor room, there came the sound of a window being opened and thrown up. An angry voice was heard.

'You *must* have broken the window yourselves! Who else could do it? There's no one in the grounds at all!'

Pat stealthily parted the leaves of the bush and stared upwards at the open window. A woman was leaning out, looking all around. Behind her pressed two other people – and Pat's heart gave a sudden jump.

The other two were David and Faith, the twins! There wasn't any doubt of it at all, because both were red-heads – and it was two fiery heads that craned over the woman's shoulders. She pushed them back roughly.

'You'll be punished for this,' she said in a sharp voice, and crashed the window down again. Tessa and Pat didn't dare to move; but as there came no further sound or movement, Pat whispered in Tessa's ear:

'Let's wait here. The twins know jolly well *they* didn't break the window – and as soon as that woman has gone out of the room I bet they'll open the window and peer out to see who threw the stone. We'll wait.'

So they waited patiently, and after about ten minutes they heard the squeak of the window being very cautiously opened. Pat parted the leaves and looked through the bush. Both twins were now hanging out of the window trying to see out as far as ever they could.

Pat remembered the little whistling call that he and Tessa had used the summer before when they had gone to fetch the twins out to play. He whistled the signal softly but clearly, sounding rather like a bird.

The twins above were transfixed with surprise. They almost fell out of the window trying to see into the bushes below. Pat whistled again.

And back came David's answering whistle, just as it used to do the summer before: 'Tui, tui, tui, too! Tuiti, too!'

Then there was a whispered conversation

between the twins and Faith disappeared. David remained at the window, whistling softly occasionally, and answered cautiously by Pat below.

At last Faith came back, looked out and then dropped a ball of screwed-up paper. By good luck it fell near the bush where Tessa and Pat were hiding, too afraid to allow themselves to be seen. Pat reached out a cautious hand and picked up the ball of paper.

Faith saw it disappear under the bush, and whispered excitedly to David, who squinted down at the bush in great curiosity. Pat opened the screwed-up paper with trembling hands.

Faith had scribbled a note to them, her writing wobbling with hurry and excitement.

I say, is it really you? We knew your whistle at once. How did you find us? We're PRISONERS here! I'm sure of it.

We were told by Miss Lawley before we went that we were to be taken to somewhere very secret because our guardians were afraid we might be kidnapped because of our money — and the awful ruby! But we think we've been kidnapped, anyway.

Someone has double-crossed our guardians, and here we are, tucked away where nobody can find us — except you. I say, you are clever. Any plans?

Faith

Tessa and Pat read the note together, amazed and shocked. They looked at one another.

'But what can we *do*?' whispered Pat. 'Go home and tell Mother, I suppose – or the police.'

'No,' said Tessa. 'Not till we've had a talk with the twins. Look, Pat – if they really *have* been kidnapped, it's been done by bad and desperate men. They might – they might do something awful to the twins if they thought they were discovered. As soon as they saw people at the front gate, demanding to be let in, they would have plenty of time to cover up all signs that Faith and David had been here – and hide the ruby, too, if they've got it. Then the twins might never be heard of again.'

This was a very long speech and Pat listened to it in silence. He thought about it.

'I think you're right,' he said, at last. 'But if we don't tell Mother or the police, what else is there to do?'

'Could we possibly rescue them ourselves?' whispered Tessa. 'If we could get them out of the house somehow, they could easily climb over that gap in the wall – and come home with us. That would be the best thing to do.'

'What about the ruby?' asked Pat.

'Oh, who cares about that?' whispered Tessa. 'It's the twins we want. Can you write a note, wrap it round a stone and throw it up into the open window?'

'You write it and I'll throw it,' said Pat. 'Tell them we'll be back tomorrow. That woman may be suspicious today. Tell them to listen for our whistle.'

Tessa took out a little diary she always kept in her pocket and scribbled Pat's message on one of the pages. He found a stone and wrapped the little page round it. It kept coming undone, so he took his shoe-lace and tied the note firmly to the stone. Now to throw it!

He stood behind the bush and took very careful aim. The stone flew straight up and in at the open window!'

'Jolly good, Pat,' whispered Tessa. 'Now, for goodness' sake, let's go. I shall feel much happier when I'm on the other side of the wall!'

7 Back home - and a fine plan

Tessa and Pat made their way cautiously through the tangled bushes and trees to the place where they had climbed over the wall. They clambered up the tree whose branch almost touched the wall, swung to the top where the spiked bricks had fallen away, and then shinned down the half-fallen tree the other side.

'I'm glad we're safely over,' said Pat, still in a whisper. 'Let's get back to our bikes.'

'No. Let's sit down under a bush and have our dinner,' said Tessa. 'We can see that lovely little secret lake with its dear little island from here. How I'd like to camp in a place like that!'

'Wouldn't it be safer to go back to our bikes?' said Pat. He had had quite enough of Brinkin Hill for one day.

'No. Oh, blow, yes – we'll have to fetch our food, of course, and it's in our baskets,' said Tessa. 'You go and fetch it, Pat, and I'll find a nice place to sit.'

Pat went off grumbling. What a nuisance girls were, always wanting their own way! He came back with the food and found Tessa sitting half under a big broom bush, whose flowers were now over. She was gazing down at the little lake.

'I do like it,' she said to Pat. 'I'd love to go and explore down there. Could we?'

'No, we couldn't,' said Pat shortly. 'It's almost two o'clock already – no wonder we're starving! And I don't mind telling you that as soon as we've finished we're biking down to get a drink at that village shop – a lovely long cool drink.'

Tessa changed her mind about exploring when she thought of the long cool drink. The two sat together and ate fast, talking over the morning's happenings with their mouths full, there was such a lot to say.

When they had finished, they went back round the wall to their bicycles, gave a last glance at the great strong gate, and set off down the flinty lane. They decided to walk, not to ride, because the hill was really very steep, and there were so many flints and ruts. They were hot and thirstier than ever when they arrived at the village shop.

'You don't get many strangers here, I suppose,' said Tessa, to the old woman who served them.

'Oh no – we'm right off the main road, here,' said the old lady. 'Why, I haven't seen a strange face till yours today, not for four months, maybe!'

The children looked at one another, thinking the same thought. Whoever had gone to Brinkin Towers had gone another way, then – a secret way! They obviously didn't want to be seen.

'Who owns Brinkin Towers now?' said Pat.

'Oh, they say it belongs to a rich man who lives far away over the seas,' said the old woman. 'Anyways, seems he's forgotten all about it now. One of these days it will fall into rack and ruin, the rain will get into the roof and owls and rats will live in it, nobody else. But don't you go there, now – I've warned you. It's a queer place, and had queer goings-on long ago. For all we know, there's queer things still going on!'

Little did she know how right she was! The children almost chuckled. They handed back their bottles and went off again, feeling better.

They sauntered back to their house, and found soon after their dinner. Then they biked home for a bathe. It was hotter than ever.

They sauntered back to their house, and found their mother hurrying and scurrying about.

'Oh, there you are!' she called. 'Did you have a nice day? Oh dear, it's a perfect nuisance, but Daddy has just telephoned down from London to say that Auntie Dora has broken her leg and will I go up and see to her household for her, for a few days.'

'What about *us*? We haven't got to go, too, have we?' asked Tessa in alarm.

'Oh no. You'd only be in the way,' said Mother. 'I wondered if you could manage for a few days by yourselves – perhaps take the tent and camp out somewhere, as it's so very hot. There's plenty of food in the house – and you can always go to a shop for a meal. I shan't be away very long.'

The two children cheered up at once. Thank goodness they need not leave the blue sea and go back to London in this hot weather!

'Camp out! It would be *heavenly*!' said Pat. 'Can we choose our own camping-place, Mother?'

'Yes,' said his busy mother, quite unsuspectingly. 'Take your tent and ground-sheet. Perhaps you can go and camp in that field where all the other children are camping out this week – they would be company for you. I'll ask Mrs Hall next door to keep an eye on you, too – you can go to her if you want anything.'

But Tessa and Pat had other ideas. As soon as they had a minute alone they spoke to one another exultingly.

'We'll go and camp on that secret lake, on the little island!' said Tessa. 'And I'm sure we'll be able to think out a fine plan for rescuing Faith and David if we've a few days to do it in.'

'Right,' said Pat, finding the secret lake suddenly very tempting, 'Fancy, Tessa – we'll be able to slip into the water a hundred times a day – and I bet that lake will be as warm as toast!'

'Gosh – what fun!' said Tessa. 'Poor Auntie Dora – I'm awfully sorry she's broken her leg – but if she *had* to do it, she couldn't have chosen a better time!'

'We'll pack everything tomorrow, early,' said Pat. 'And I've no doubt when Mother comes back again she'll find four children here to welcome her, instead of two!'

8 Off on a real adventure

Tessa and Pat said goodbye to their mother the next morning, and then set to work to pack up their own kit.

'Tent – ground-sheet – food – rug – bathing suits – towel,' recited Tessa. 'Tooth-brushes – soap – hair-brush – comb – come on, you think of something, too, Pat.'

It didn't really take very long to get ready. The two of them fixed boxes to the backs of their bicycles and piled everything into them, as well as into their baskets. They also took kit-bags, and, by the time they had finished, their bicycles seemed twice as heavy as usual to pedal along.

'Have you packed the tin-opener and the bottle opener?' sang out Pat as they started. 'There, I knew you wouldn't think of important things like those. You go and pack crowds of tins and never even *think* of bringing something to open them.'

'I can't think of *every*thing,' said Tessa. 'You

can jolly well go back and get those yourself!'

They really were ready to start off at last. Away they went, more slowly than the day before because of their heavy load. What fun to be heading straight into an adventure like this! And nobody knew!

They cycled through Corfe Castle and took the turning to Brinkin village. They stopped at the little shop to collect plenty of bottles of lemonade and ginger-beer.

'My, you're going to have a fine time!' said the old lady, seeing their packages. 'Where are you going to camp?'

'Oh, somewhere near water so that we can bathe,' answered Pat, at once, before Tessa could say too much. 'See you again sometime!'

They went off quickly and soon came to the steep Brinkin Hill. They wondered if there was a better way to the secret lake, but decided that there wasn't, or surely there would be some signpost to it, it was such a beauty spot. They had better stick to the way they knew.

So they laboured panting up the hill till they came to the fast-shut gates. Then they wheeled their bicycles painfully through the undergrowth as they skirted the wall. At last they came to where a path led down to the lake. They debated what to do. Should they get over the wall and try to speak to the twins first – or find a camping-place on the island?

'Let's hope there'll be a boat there,' said Pat, 'or I can see us swimming with bundles tied to the tops of our head, like native women do in Africa!'

'There must be some way of getting to the island,' said Tessa. 'People must once have gone across to the building we saw there.'

Pat decided to go over the wall and see if the twins answered to his whistle. He was soon hiding in a bush under the broken window. He whistled softly, and then, feeling braver, a little more loudly. There was no answer at all.

The window was shut, though still broken, and there was no face looking out. The twins must be somewhere else.

Well, it was no use waiting. He might as well go back to Tessa and help her down to the secret little island with all their luggage. Perhaps it would be a good idea to come back at night when there would be no danger at all of being seen.

Tessa was delighted to see him, but disappointed to hear that he hadn't spoken with the twins. She agreed that it would be the best thing to get down to the island and find a camping-place – and to go back to Brinkin Towers when it was dark. There would be a moon to help them then.

They made their way down the steep hill to the little lake. They were weighed down with all their things and had to go very slowly indeed, because although there were steps cut out of the rocky hillside, they were overgrown, and worn by the weather. It was difficult to balance all their goods and watch their step at the same time.

At last they were down by the lake-side. The water was smooth, clear and very blue. The little island lay some way off, looking most inviting. The children could just see its queer little towers behind the trees that grew there.

'This looks like a boat-house,' said Pat, going off towards a broken-down, weather-beaten shed, built out half-way over the water, on piles. The door at the back was broken, and Pat stepped inside.

'There *is* a boat!' he said. 'And it must still be all right, because it's floating! What mouldy old cushions inside! They smell horrid.'

They found a couple of paddles hanging up. There were no oars to be seen, but as the boat was a very small one, that didn't matter.

'Spread out the ground-sheet in the boat and we'll put all the goods on that,' said Tessa. That was soon done. Then the two stepped gingerly into the boat and took a paddle each.

'It can't possibly matter using this old boat,' said Pat, as he undid a half-rotten rope from a post. 'Anyway, for all we know, it belongs to David and Faith for the time being, if Brinkin Towers has been rented for them. Here goes!'

The boat was paddled out of its shed and into the hot sunshine. Lovely! Over the blue water went the two children, their boat now moving quite fast.

'Look out – we're coming into shore,' said Pat. 'Island ahead – and here's a perfect little cove to pull into. Might be made for us!'

'Well, here we are,' said Tessa, gazing at the little island. 'It's the very first time I've ever spent a night on an island – I hope we shall enjoy it!'

9 On the little island

The two children pulled the boat up on to the sandy shore of the cove and then landed their goods.

'Now we'll go and find a good place to camp,' said Pat. 'I wonder if anyone ever comes here. It doesn't look like it!'

They wandered over the island. It was very much overgrown, but at one time must have been laid out partly as a garden, for the children could still see roses flowering high in brambly bushes.

Then they suddenly came to the queer little building they had seen from the top of the hill. It was set in a grove of foreign-looking trees that had been planted in a square.

Inside the square stood the long, low building. Pat thought it looked like a temple. It had quaint towers, delicate and pointed – Pat said they must be minarets, but he wasn't sure. They didn't look like English towers, anyway.

The windows were a queer shape too, and the steps that led up to the beautifully carved door were set with curious bits of coloured glass – dirty now, but gleaming here and there where one or two had been cleaned by heavy rain.

The children stood still, listening, feeling somehow that somebody must be there. But there was nobody, of course. They went up the steps and pushed the beautifully carved door, but it was locked. They went to look in at the windows.

'Why, it's a kind of museum inside,' said Tessa, beginning to speak in a whisper again. 'What are all those queer figures, Pat?'

'Idols, I should think,' said Pat. 'Indian idols. See how they sit cross-legged and stare into space.'

A horrid thought suddenly struck Tessa. *Indian* idols! Why – wasn't it from India that the Strange Ruby had come? And hadn't the old woman in the shop said that she thought Brinkin Towers once belonged to a rich man from over the seas? Suppose – just suppose – he was an Indian and this place was his.

'And just suppose,' said Tessa, speaking out loud, 'just suppose that the Indians want to get their sacred stone back again! If they kidnapped the owners, who are Faith and David, wouldn't they bring them here to Brinkin Towers, the house that belonged to Indians? My goodness – I'm beginning to understand things now.'

'What in the world are you talking about?' said Pat, in astonishment.

Tessa told him. 'It all fits in, you see,' she said when she had finished. 'I don't know how they managed to take Faith and David away like this – but it's the ruby they want, there's no doubt about that. I expect it once belonged to an image rather like these.'

They peered in at the window again. Tessa shivered. The grinning figures sat there so still, their ugly faces motionless, their jewelled eyes staring.

They tiptoed round all the windows, peering into the rooms. It certainly did seem like a museum, for not only the carved figures were there, but great vases, wonderful carved swords, beautiful little statues, and hangings that had once been rich and magnificent.

'Pat – this window has come loose,' said Tessa, startled, as the window her face was pressed against suddenly swung inwards. 'Anyone could get in here, look – it's a wonder no thieves have been inside.'

'Well, for one thing they wouldn't know there was such a place here,' said Pat, 'all hidden away and secret – and for another I should think the ordinary tramp would be scared stiff. I feel a bit wobbly myself.'

Tessa pulled at the window and tried to close it, but the hasp was broken. She caught sight of

53

an image just inside, staring at her with bright emerald eyes, and she scowled at him.

'Don't you glare at me like that,' she said, fiercely.

But, as he seemed to scowl back, she hurriedly went away to join Pat. Carved images that scowled were decidedly not suited to a brilliant August day.

They found a lovely place to camp, in a little glade. Through the trees they could see the blue water of the lake. Sunshine freckled the ground, and when the wind blew gently the freckles danced. It was really lovely.

'We won't go up to Brinkin Towers till it's dark,' said Pat, taking off his clothes to bathe. 'Where are my bathing drawers? Oh, there they are. Coming, Tessa?'

'I'm just going to arrange things a bit,' said Tessa. 'When shall we put up the tent, Pat? Or do you think we need? Couldn't we just sleep on the ground-sheet and rug tonight? It's so frightfully hot.'

'Let's not bother about the tent,' said Pat. 'Let's just have the sky for a ceiling, and grass for a bed.'

'We promised Mother we'd use the ground-sheet,' said Tessa, who always kept her word.

'All right. We'll lie on that and the rug,' said Pat. 'Now I'm going into the water!' And away he went through the trees, a lithe brown figure, and flung himself into the lake-water with a tremendous splash. Lovely!

Tessa soon followed, and the two had a wonderful swim. The lake water was deep a little way from the island, but wonderfully clear. Near to the island the bed of the lake was soft and sandy.

'Now we'll go and lie in the sun and get dry,' said Pat. 'And eat a most enormous lunch. You know I'm very sorry for grown-ups, Tessa – it must be horrid not to feel hungry all the time, like we do!'

They had a wonderful day and sat and watched the sun sink down in a sky of brilliant rose-pink and orange. It didn't even get chilly when the sun had quite gone.

'When shall we go up to the house?' said Tessa, about ten o'clock, waking up from a doze. 'I shall fall fast asleep in a minute or two. Had we better go soon? It's almost dark now.'

'There's the moon coming up,' said Pat. 'We may as well start now. Here's good luck to us, Tessa – and for goodness' sake go quietly!'

10 Inside Brinkin Towers

Tessa and Pat went to the little cove, which was now streaked with moonlight, and Tessa stepped into the boat. Pat pushed off, and then leapt in himself. The children paddled in silence across to the mainland. It was a beautiful night, and almost as light as day.

They tied the boat up quietly, and then made their way up the steep path to Brinkin Towers. Once at the top they walked carefully round the wall till they came to where they could climb over.

Up the tree, on to the broken wall-top, down the tree the other side – and there they were standing in the grounds once more. An owl hooted and made them both jump almost out of their skins.

'Come on – I believe I can see a light in that second floor room, where the twins were yesterday,' whispered Pat. They made their way over to the great house and looked up.

The curtains were drawn over the window,

but through the crack shone a light. Were the twins there alone? The two children did hope so!

'I'm going to whistle very softly,' said Pat. 'I daren't do it loudly in case anyone is with the twins. But they both have very sharp ears, so if I whistle almost under my breath they'll hear me!'

He waited, listening, for a moment. Then he whistled softly. 'Tui-tui-tui-too. Tuitui-too.'

Holding their breath, the two waited in silence. Nothing happened for a moment or two – then the curtains were cautiously drawn a little way apart, and a head peeped out.

A very soft whistle came in answer. Then something dropped down from the window, nicking Pat's ear as it passed. The curtains were pulled close again, so that the light showed through just a tiny crack, as before.

On the ground beside Pat lay a key, with a small label attached to it. He picked it up, surprised.

'There's a message on the label,' whispered Pat, and he and Tessa screwed up their eyes and tried to read it by moonlight.

The message was in Faith's writing.

Key of garden door, round other side of house, read Pat. *We got it by a trick today. Can you come in, creep up to our room and unlock our door? The key of our room is in the lock on the outside, we know.*

57

Hope you don't get caught! We'll push a piece of paper just under our door, so that you'll see it sticking out and know it's our room.

Faith

The two stared at one another, delighted and half-scared. They could get into the house – that is, if the garden door was only locked and not bolted! They could make their way upstairs, and unlock the twins' door – and then escape would be easy!

'Come along – let's find that garden door,' whispered Tessa. They went cautiously round the house, glad that where once gravel paths had been there were now only weeds and grass. Their footsteps could not possibly be heard.

On the other side of the house was a little side-door.

'This must be the one,' whispered Pat, and he slid the key into the lock. It turned easily, fortunately, without even a squeak. Now – was it bolted as well as locked? He pushed hard – and the door opened! What a bit of luck!

They crept into a dark passage, unlighted by the moon. Pat paused and Tessa bumped into him.

'I'm just trying to get my bearings,' he whispered. 'Let me see – the twins' room is on the other side of the house. Let's find the stairs and go up.'

'There may be a backstairs,' whispered Tessa. 'It would be safer to go up those than the main stairs.'

'Good idea,' said Pat. He crept forward cautiously, and soon came into a dimly lighted hall, a great place full of enormous pieces of old furniture and heavy hangings. Black shadows lurked in the far corners, and Pat couldn't help wondering if anyone was hiding there, waiting for him. His knees began to feel a bit shaky.

Rooms opened off the hall. One room had its door slightly ajar, and a beam of light streamed out. That was clearly a room to be avoided. Where was the kitchen? If there was no one there, they might find the backstairs and creep up.

A green baize door showed in a far corner.

'That must be the way to the kitchen,' Pat whispered in Tessa's ear. 'Come on – quietly as you can.'

They both had on rubber shoes, and made no noise as they tiptoed over the thick carpets to the green baize door in the corner. It was a swing door with no lock or latch. Pat pushed at it carefully.

Behind was a short passage, and at the end, showing very dimly in the light from the hall, was another door. The children let the baize door swing slowly into place, and then, in the darkness, felt their way to the other door. That also was a swing door. Pat, his knees still trembling, pushed it a little way open. At once a noise came to his ears – somebody snoring!

He pushed the door wider open, and through the crack caught sight of two things – a big fat woman lying back in a wicker chair, asleep and snoring – and a flight of backstairs just behind her, leading to the first floor!

He shut the door and whispered into Tessa's ear what he had seen.

'Shall we risk waking the woman, and make for the backstairs?' he said.

'Yes,' said Tessa, her knees beginning to shake, too. 'Come on, Pat – nothing venture, nothing have!'

11 A shock for Pat

Pat tiptoed round the door into the vast kitchen. The woman still snored on, her mouth open. Tessa followed. The two skirted the big kitchen carefully, keeping an eye on the woman. She must be the cook, they decided.

Just as they crept behind her, a dreadful thing happened. Pat didn't see a cat under the woman's chair, but the cat saw him. It leapt out at him playfully, and he fell over it. Down he went, and bumped into the back of the woman's chair.

Tessa was terrified. She was by the window curtains, heavy blue ones that reached to the ground. She slid behind them just as the woman jumped up heavily from her chair.

Pat was up and running for the backstairs when she saw him.

'HEY, YOU!' the woman shouted. 'What are you doing? Who are you?'

But Pat had disappeared upstairs, leaving

Tessa behind the curtains in the kitchen. Blow, blow, blow – what a maddening thing to happen!

The woman was too fat to chase Pat up the stairs and catch him, but she soon gave the alarm. She caught up a hand-bell from a table, and shook it vigorously.

Jangle-JANGLE-JANGLE!

Tessa trembled behind the curtains. Whatever would happen now?

Plenty happened almost at once. Two men came racing out to the kitchen, shouting out something in a foreign language. They were brown-faced, small, and looked fierce. They shouted in English to the cook.

'Now what is this?' cried one man.

'A boy! He went up there,' said the cook. 'I saw him.'

The man said something rapidly to the other man. Tessa could not understand a word. Then one man sped up the backstairs and the other ran back to the hall, apparently to go up the front stairs, and so cut the boy off, wherever he was. Nobody knew that Tessa was behind the curtains.

Tessa stood trembling there, wondering if they would find Pat. It wasn't long before she knew. She suddenly heard shouts from the men, and then Pat's voice.

'You let go my arm, you beast. You're hurting me!'

Tessa wanted to go to Pat's help – but what was the good of that? She would simply be taken prisoner, too. So she stayed where she was, very much afraid. The fat woman sank down into her wicker chair again, muttering. Tessa could hear the chair creak beneath her weight.

Upstairs, poor Pat was having a rough time. He had darted up the backstairs like a monkey and on to a small narrow landing. He had made for the first door he saw, and it had opened on to a big landing.

On the opposite side he could see another flight of stairs, wide and sweeping – they must be the front stairs, leading down into the hall. If he could slip down those, he could make his way to the garden door and escape!

But a small dark man came up the stairs just as he ran to the top. He looked like a foreigner and Pat darted back – straight into the arms of the fellow who had slipped up the backstairs. He was caught!

He began to yell as the man caught his arms, and twisted them behind his back. 'You let go my arm, you beast. You're hurting me!'

The two men were soon joined by two more. All but one looked like foreigners, and one of them even wore a turban, and looked much more stately than the others. The fourth man seemed to be English by his looks and his speech.

'Who are you?' said the turbaned man. Pat made no answer.

'Let's take him up to the other kids and see if they know him,' said the fourth man, who spoke English well. 'How did he get in? There's something funny about this.'

Pat was dragged up another flight of stairs, and came to a big door. It was locked and the key was in the lock. The turbaned man turned it, and opened the door. He pushed Pat inside at once.

'Pat!' shouted two delighted voices. 'Pat! You've come!'

'Sh,' said Pat, afraid that the unsuspecting twins would ask where Tessa was. He didn't want the men to know there had been anyone with him. The four men came round the door. The Englishman spoke to the twins.

'So he's a friend of yours, is he? Who is he? How did he know you were here?'

Pat frowned at the twins, and they guessed they were not to give him away. They looked innocently at the four frowning men.

'Didn't *you* tell him we were here? Perhaps our new governess, Miss Twisley, did. Can he stay and play with us?'

'Pah!' said the man. He turned to one of the foreigners and spoke sharply to him. 'Fetch Miss Twisley here. She may know this boy.'

In two or three minutes a sharp-faced woman came in. She eyed Pat in surprise.

'Who's he?' she said to the watching men. 'Why have you brought *him* here?'

'Don't you know him?' asked the turbaned man. She shook her head, puzzled. Pat didn't like her at all. She had a hard, mean face, with lips so thin that they could hardly be seen.

There was a short consultation between all five in some foreign language. Then the Englishman turned to the three waiting children.

'We shall leave you here for the night – and if you don't talk in the morning, and tell us how this boy knew you were here, you'll be very sorry for yourselves.'

The children said nothing, but watched the men go out with Miss Twisley. The door closed, the key turned in the lock. Prisoners again – but at least there were three of them now – and Tessa was somewhere loose in the house!

12 What shall Tessa do?

As soon as the footsteps had died away, and the children were alone, they turned eagerly to one another. Pat put his finger to his lips.

'Be careful what you say,' he whispered, 'one of them may have been left outside the door to listen. Look – let's come over to the window, and get behind those thick curtains – they won't be able to hear a word we say, then.'

Queer stories were exchanged behind the curtains! The twins told Pat that when their old governess, Miss Lawley, left, another one had been engaged – she must have belonged to the same gang as the kidnappers, because it was she who had arranged to take them away.

'We were to go on holiday somewhere lovely, so she said,' whispered David. 'But she wouldn't tell us where. The car came – and off we went – but we were taken *here* instead of somewhere lovely! We just managed to overhear Miss Twisley telephoning once and caught the name "Bringking Hill" – at least, that's what it sounded like – and we had to hope you would eventually get the letter we threw out of the car.'

'Yes, we did,' said Pat. 'And we discovered that Brinkin Hill – not Bringking as you thought – was quite near Swanage, where we've come for our holiday again – so we did a bit of snooping round on our own, and found the place – and you!'

'Jolly good work,' said Faith. 'We think we must have been given a sleeping-draught, or something, because we fell absolutely sound asleep in the car, and when we woke up, we were in this room! It's our bedroom, as well as our playroom.'

Pat had already seen two beds there. A thought struck him. 'How on earth did you get the key of that garden door?' he asked. 'We slipped in easily with it.'

'Well, Miss Twisley took us out in the grounds for a walk round,' said David. 'Through that door, of course. And when we came back, she locked it carefully behind us – but left the key in the door! Faith pretended to fall over a rug in the hall and hurt her knee and yelled so frightfully that Miss Twisley took her attention off me for a moment – and I whizzed back to the door and took the key. Easy!'

'Jolly fine,' said Pat, admiringly. 'I say – are these foreign fellows holding you for ransom, or something? Do they want the ruby?'

'I suppose so. We don't really know,' said

Faith. 'Pat – where's Tessa? Did she come with you? You said "we" just now when you spoke about getting in through the garden door.'

'Tessa is somewhere in the house!' said Pat. 'She hid when I got caught. Goodness knows where she is. I only hope she'll escape before they find her and give the alarm. Then we'll all be rescued.'

'Where can she be, I wonder?' said Faith. 'She must be scared, hiding all by herself.'

Tessa certainly was scared. She had stood shivering behind the blue curtains for what seemed a very long while. The woman was still in the kitchen, so Tessa simply didn't dare to try and escape.

Suddenly she heard footsteps coming down the little passage that led from hall to kitchen. The door swung open and the four men came in. The woman stood up at once.

The men snapped some questions at her about Pat, but she could tell them nothing, except that she had been asleep, had been awakened by the noise of someone falling behind her, had sprung up and seen Pat running up the backstairs.

'We shall have to take the children somewhere else immediately!' said the Englishman. 'If this boy, Pat, knows enough to come here, then others may know what he knows, too. But *how* did he know? Well, we'll make them talk in the morning.'

'Where shall we take them to hide, then?' asked one of the men.

The turbaned man answered at once in his own language and everyone nodded. Tessa strained her ears, but she couldn't understand what the man had said. Oh dear – were they really going to take Faith and David somewhere else – and Pat, too, this time? If only she could escape and give the alarm!

'But by the time I've escaped, got home, and raised the alarm, these men will have spirited the others away,' she thought, dismally. 'And I'm not sure I could get over that wall from this side without Pat's help. I'm sure I couldn't!'

She listened again to the men talking and

picked up a few bits of news. Faith and David *had* been kidnapped – and their ransom was the *Strange Ruby*! If the Ruby was not delivered to them, according to their instructions, then the children would never be heard of again!

'And once more ill-fortune will have followed the owners of the ruby,' thought poor Tessa. 'Oh dear – this is like a bad dream.'

She listened again. The Englishman was speaking now, half in a foreign tongue, half in his own language. Apparently he was urging the turbaned man to send someone to steal the ruby – according to him, it could be done, if his plan was followed.

'Time is valuable,' urged the man. 'If we can get the ruby at once, by using my plan, then why not? What is the point of messing about with the children, and holding things up?'

'It is bad luck to steal the Strange Ruby,' said the turbaned man. 'It should always be given from one person to another. But maybe we shall have to get it your way, Williams. I do not know.'

They went out of the kitchen. The fat woman muttered and groaned. She lighted a candle, and blew out the oil lamp on the table. Then she went mumbling up the backstairs, leaving the kitchen in darkness.

Now was Tessa's chance. What, oh what, was the best thing to do?

13 Tessa does well

It didn't take Tessa long to make up her mind. She felt sure she wouldn't be able to climb back over the wall without Pat's helping hand – and, anyway, by the time she got help it would be morning or later, and there was the chance that all three of the others would have been spirited away into thin air.

'Goodness knows where those awful men would take them to,' thought Tessa, desperately. 'To the other side of the world perhaps – and we might never hear of them again. I'd be the only one left – how dreadful!'

She peeped between the curtains into the dark kitchen. There was no moonlight there, and except for a glow from an oilstove on which the cook had left something simmering, there was no light at all.

Tessa made up her mind to wait till everyone had gone to bed – then she would creep up the stairs by herself, find the room where Faith, David and Pat were imprisoned, and let them out!

'That is, if the key's on the outside of the door!' she thought. 'What I shall do if it isn't, I simply don't know!'

She wondered how late it was – half past eleven? Midnight? She really didn't know. She came out from behind the curtain and wondered if there was a better hiding place.

She tiptoed to the door that led out to the hall. A pat on her ankle made her jump violently.

She rushed back to the curtains, and then scolded herself. It was only that playful cat, of course! She had nearly yelled in fright when it had jumped out and patted her foot. She really must be more careful.

She tiptoed to the door again, and the cat leapt around her, asking her to play with him. But Tessa had no time for play! In fact, she felt very cross with the cat for tripping up Pat, and causing him to be caught.

She slipped out of the door into the little passage that led to the baize door. She opened this very cautiously, and peeped through the crack. The hall was quiet and deserted, lit dimly as before.

Next to the baize door was a cupboard. Tessa thought it would be a good idea to creep into it.

She could sit down then, and have a rest, till she decided it was late enough to go and find the others.

She went into the cupboard. It was full of coats and boots. She pulled some of the coats down to the floor and snuggled into them. Then she waited. She fell asleep, of course! She was tired, and everything was very quiet. The coats were soft and warm. Tessa's eyes closed, her head fell forward, and she slept peacefully.

She awoke with a jump. Somehow the cat had followed her, and had now made its way into the cupboard by inserting its paw in the door-crack and then wriggling itself through. Purring loudly, it was now on Tessa's knee, pushing its claws in and out of her jeans.

She was wide awake at once, and luckily did not cry out.

'Oh, it's you again,' she whispered to the cat. 'Stop digging your claws into me – but thank you for waking me. Goodness – how long have I been asleep?'

She crept out of the cupboard into the hall. It was still dimly lighted. There was not a sound to be heard anywhere. It *felt* very late, Tessa thought. Actually it was about two o'clock – she had slept for over two hours.

She went softly up the wide stairs, and came out on to a landing. All was quiet. No lights were to be seen anywhere, except the dim light on the landing.

Up she went again to the second floor, trying to make out which side of the house the twins' room should be. She came to a door – and in the dim light of the landing lamp, she caught sight of a piece of paper sticking out from beneath the bottom edge of one of the doors facing her!

She remembered that Faith had said in her message that they would mark their room in that way. They had remembered, and here was the mark! This must be the right room.

The key was on her side of the door – thank goodness for that! If only, only it was the right door! She bent down and tried to see if there was a light shining through the keyhole, but of course, the key was in and she could see nothing. She didn't dare to take it out, in case it rattled.

She tried the door cautiously. It was locked. She turned the key. It squeaked a little and she stood still in fright. But nobody came, nobody called out!

She unlocked the door completely, and turned the handle. She opened the door and crept swiftly round it, shutting it quietly behind her.

A voice at once spoke from the darkness of the room. 'Who's that?'

It was Pat's voice! Tessa could have cried with joy.

'It's me, Tessa,' she whispered. 'I've unlocked the door. Are Faith and David here? Let's be quick and go before anyone comes!'

'The twins are asleep,' came Pat's low voice. 'I didn't let myself sleep – I was so hoping you might come. Good old Tessa! We'll wake the twins and escape.'

Pat switched on a little torch. He woke the twins quietly and they sat up at once.

'Tessa's here,' whispered Pat. 'She's unlocked the door from the outside. Let's go quickly. We're all dressed, so we don't need to wait for anything!'

Shaking with excitement and delight, the twins went to the door with Pat and Tessa. They stood outside on the landing for a moment, and then Pat led the way very cautiously.

'We'll go out of that garden door,' he whispered. 'Now – not a sound, anyone. Come on!'

14 Escape to the island

The four children went softly along the landing and came to the head of the stairs. They went down, glad that there was such a thick stair-carpet to muffle their footsteps. They were soon on the first floor.

Then down to the hall they crept. Pat led the way to the garden door, wondering whether the men had discovered that they had left the key on the outside!

They apparently hadn't – but they had bolted the door on the inside, so someone had evidently discovered that it was not locked, and, not having been able to find the key, had bolted the door.

It was a matter of a second or two to unbolt the door and slip out. The moon was still brilliant, though in the south-west some big banked-up clouds were gathering.

'It's going to pour soon,' said Pat. 'It looks like a storm – and hark, that's thunder, isn't it?'

'Yes,' said Tessa, as she heard a rumble. 'We can't go scrambling over the countryside at night in a storm – especially as we have only two bicycles. I think we'd better go down to that little hidden island on the secret lake for the rest of the night. Nobody would ever guess we were there. Let's spend the night there.'

Pat thought it was a good idea. They were all tired out with excitement and strain, and longing to rest and sleep. So without more ado they made their way to the wall, climbed over and then struggled down the steep hill, glad of the moonlight to light the way.

They jumped into the little boat and paddled sleepily off to the island.

'This boat's leaking,' said Faith, feeling her feet suddenly wet.

'It's because there are four of us and we're heavy,' said Pat, though Tessa couldn't see why weight should make the boat leak. But she was too tired to argue, and hardly felt the water coming into her shoes as she and Pat paddled valiantly across to the little island.

They heard a clap of thunder as they landed, and it made them all jump. 'Look at that enormous black cloud coming up,' said Faith. 'It will soon blot out the moon. I bet there's going to be a terrific storm. We shall get soaked. Is there anywhere to shelter on the island?'

A large, fierce plop of rain struck Pat on the

head. Then another and another. Yes, certainly they would all be soaked! He thought of the queer little temple with its silent figures. Could they shelter there?

'Tessa – do you think we'd better climb through that unfastened window into the temple where those images are?' he asked. 'We could shelter there for the night. I can't see that it would matter, sleeping there. Nobody seems to bother about the place now.'

The moon was suddenly swept behind the black cloud and at once everywhere was dark. Pat switched on his torch.

'Better take the rug and the ground-sheet and the food and everything into the temple too,' he said. 'They'll all be soaked if we don't.'

The wind got up and blew loudly. More rain came, spiteful rain that stung their faces and hands. Hurriedly they collected everything from the little glade and ran for the queer building.

'Shelter in the port till I climb in at the window and open the door,' said Pat. So they stood there, shivering, while he clambered in through the swinging window and went to the door.

But he couldn't open the door, and had to open a big window nearby instead. They all climbed in, and handed the various belongings to Pat. He set them on the floor, and then flashed his torch

round the room. The twins exclaimed in surprise at the sight of the grinning figures.

'What frightful creatures! I don't think I like them,' said Faith. 'Gosh – have we got to sleep with them grinning and staring at us all the time?'

'They won't hurt us,' said Tessa. 'They're no more than great dolls! My word – listen to the storm now! I *am* glad we didn't try to battle all the way home in this. We'd never have got there!'

'I'm going to light this funny little oil lamp,' said Pat, who had found a queer-shaped one on a table. 'That's if it still has oil in. Yes – it has, good. A little light on the scene will help us!'

But it didn't, really! It just made the idols look rather lifelike, because the light shone on their jewelled eyes and made them gleam and shine.

'Not very nice company,' said Pat, flinging himself down on the rug. 'Come on, everyone. Let's lie down and try to get a bit of sleep!'

Tessa found a few mats to make the floor softer, but they were all very uncomfortable indeed. Nobody could go to sleep, especially as the wind howled round like a mad thing, and draughts blew in everywhere. Great torrents of rain pattered on the roof, and the thunder rumbled round.

The lightning flashed now and again, and

nobody felt at all happy. They shivered with only one rug between them.

The little oil lamp flickered and went out. There had been very, very little oil in it. Now it was quite dark except for an occasional flash of lightning. But soon the storm died away, and the wind grew quieter.

It was in a quiet spell that Pat heard a curious noise. What could it be? It came from somewhere outside.

He sat up – and in a trice he knew what it was. Someone was rowing a boat – it was the sound of oars that he had heard – of course it was! Had they been discovered? Who was coming?

He roused the others, who were half-dozing. 'Someone's coming,' he said. 'I can hear the oars. They mustn't find us here – or our belongings! Quick, we must hide them – and hide ourselves, too!'

15 Secret visit

The others were wide awake at once, and Tessa looked round the strange room, scared. She couldn't at first remember where she was. The storm had now passed, and the moonlight sent its brilliant beams into the room, picking out the gleaming eyes of some of the silent images.

They all heard the click of the oars in the rowlocks of a boat.

'Who can it be?' asked Faith, in a whisper.

'I can only think it's one or more of the men from Brinkin Towers, come to hunt for us,' said Pat, desperately. 'They must have found that we've gone, and begun to search for us. I don't know why they should imagine we'd come here! Perhaps they found their boat gone, and that made them suspicious.'

'Well – they'll see it now, anyway,' said Tessa. 'They'll probably land in the same cove as we did! They'll know for certain we're here, then.'

'I wonder where they got the second boat

from,' said Pat. 'I only saw the one – and that was dirty and old – the one we took.'

'They'd be sure to have a good boat somewhere,' said David. 'They wouldn't use that mouldy old one.'

The children heard the sound of voices. Pat leapt up.

'They'll search this building,' he said. 'Let's see if there's anywhere to hide. We might as well give them a run for their money. Make them hunt about a bit!'

'Look – let's pull everything under that great table,' said Faith. 'We can drape the cloth over our things and hide them.'

'And do you see that big grinning image, sitting high up there, on that platform arrangement with a heavy gold curtain behind him?' said Pat. We could all stand behind it. Come on – I can hear the boat being pulled up now – they'll be here in a minute.'

They could hear no footsteps, but they could now hear the voices much more loudly, though they couldn't make out the words. Tessa helped Faith put everything under the big table, and then dragged down the heavy cloth that covered it, so that it hid what was underneath.

The boys were exploring behind the curtain. 'Come on,' they called to the girls. 'It's a queer curtain. It's set with tiny openwork holes – we can see through them without being seen. Hurry up!'

Just as the sound of a key came from the door
at the front of the temple, the two girls climbed
up to the little platform, and slipped behind the
heavy gold curtain. They saw at once that what
the boys had said was true – they could peer
through the tiny holes embroidered in the
material.

A voice came loudly to their ears. 'In here,
Rinji. Bring the stuff.'

It was the voice of the Englishman they had
seen with the foreigners. Each of the children put
an eye to a hole in the curtain, and watched
silently as two men came into the room.

A little dark man came in with the Englishman they knew. He was dressed in loose robes, and glanced round at the great images in fright and awe. The other man took no notice of them whatsoever.

The children braced themselves, expecting the men to search for them.

But they didn't! The two men made no hunt for them at all. Instead they did some very peculiar things indeed.

The little man, evidently a servant of some kind, carried what looked like a roll of thick cloth over his shoulder. He set it down, and the other man helped him to unroll it. The children strained their eyes at the holes in the curtain, trying to see what was happening.

The rolls of cloth appeared to be three rugs of some kind. They were set out on the floor. The little servant disappeared, and came back with a box that appeared to be very heavy indeed. He set it down with a thud that shook the room.

'Everything in there?' asked the other man, and opened the lid. 'Fetch the other box and let me have a look at that.'

Another box was brought and put down with a thud. It was duly examined and the lid shut down again. The man looked round the strange room with its curious images, carved swords and beautiful vases.

'These must be worth a mint of money,' he said. 'My word – look at that grinning, cross-legged fellow up there on the platform!'

This was the figure just in front of the curtain behind which the children were hiding. They shrank back as the man came near to the platform. He shone his torch on the face of the glittering image.

'What have *you* got to laugh at, sitting there day and night alone in this horrible place?' demanded the man. The little dark servant pulled at his sleeve nervously, evidently disapproving of such behaviour. He muttered something in a strange language. The Englishman laughed.

'You're not really afraid of *him*, are you, Rinji? Like to see me topple him over?'

Filled with real terror at such an idea, the small dark fellow turned and ran out of the room. The other man followed, laughing. In amazement the children heard the door being shut, and after some while, the sound of the boat being rowed off again over the water.

'Why didn't they hunt for us?' said Pat, bewildered.

'Why did they come here with all that stuff, whatever it is?' asked Faith. 'And what *is* the stuff? Let's come and see, now it's safe.'

They all stepped down from the platform to the ground. The moon shone brightly on the things the men had brought.

'Look at all this!' said Pat, astounded. 'How very – very – extraordinary!'

16 Unexpected gifts - and a shock

The two men had certainly left some puzzling things.

'Three thick, warm rugs, each big enough to roll round anyone two or three times,' said David, astonished.

'A box of tinned food – all kinds!' said Tessa, lifting the lid.

'And in here are bottles,' exclaimed Faith, looking into the second big box.

'What are they all *for*?' wondered David. 'Is someone coming to camp-out here?'

'Gosh – *I* know what it is!' said Pat, suddenly. 'They haven't discovered yet that we've escaped – but they've been making their plans about moving us out of Brinkin Towers, and the place they've chosen to hide us in is *here* – here in this peculiar temple building, or whatever it is!'

The others stared at him, their faces pale in the moonlight. David smacked him on the back and laughed.

'You've got it, Pat! Well, would you believe it – the kidnappers have picked on the very place to dump us in that we've chosen ourselves to hide in! I call that really funny.'

Everyone laughed. They felt suddenly much more cheerful. So their escape hadn't yet been discovered – and even when it *was* discovered, the men surely wouldn't dream of looking into the very place they themselves had prepared.

'These things they've brought are supposed to be for us – when they bring us here!' grinned Pat. 'Three rugs – because, of course, they thought there were only three of us, they haven't seen Tessa – and food enough to last for days! Honestly, it's super!'

'Looking at those tins has made me feel hungry,' said Faith. 'What about having a snack now – and I'm frightfully thirsty, too.'

'Right – we'll have a good tuck-in at the food our enemies have so kindly provided,' said Pat. 'And then, instead of tossing and turning and shivering with only one rug between us, we'll have a nice comfy sleep in the great thick rugs those fellows have given us out of the kindness of their hearts! I'm going to enjoy all this!'

'And in the morning we'll take our boat and row to the other end of the lake, find a landing-place somewhere, and make our way home,' said Faith. 'And we'll send the police after those rogues. This is a very nice adventure indeed now.'

'Don't count your chickens before they're hatched,' said David, warningly. 'You're always doing that, Faith. It may not be so easy as you think. Once those fellows know we've escaped, they'll search everywhere. We'll have to be on our guard.'

'Oh, we're all right now,' said Faith. 'Anyone got a tin-opener?'

They were soon eating tongue, hacked out of a tin with a pocket-knife, biscuits and tinned peaches, washed down with ginger-beer.

'This is just about the nicest meal I've ever had,' said Faith. 'It's all the nicer because we're eating it sitting on the floor, surrounded by those strange figures, in the very middle of the night!'

'It's not the middle of the night now,' said David, his mouth full. 'It will soon be dawn!' He yawned hugely. 'Gracious, I'm sleepy. I'll be able to sleep properly now, in those thick rugs with a good meal inside me.'

'The girls can have two of the thick rugs the men brought, and we'll have the third one and our own,' said Pat. 'Come on – let's get into them now.'

The rugs were certainly very big and cosy. It didn't take long for all four children to fall fast asleep, tired out with the night's excitement. They slept till the sun was high in the sky.

David awoke first, and lay for a minute or two, looking straight into the face of one of the images, who seemed to be watching him. The boy sat up and laughed.

'Are you thinking it's queer to have four visitors for the night?' he asked the silent figure. 'What's the time – goodness, it's almost half past nine – and what a heavenly morning!'

He awoke the others, and they all sat up, trying to remember where they were.

'I'm still sleepy,' yawned Tessa. 'What a lovely day! Let's go and have a splash in the lake before breakfast – if you think it's safe to do that, Pat.'

'Oh yes – we'll find a sheltered spot where nobody looking out from Brinkin Towers could see us,' said Pat. 'Then we'll have breakfast, find our boat, and see if we can make for the other side of the lake and get home from there.'

They ran out of the temple and came to the little cove. They looked for their boat, wondering again how it was that the men had not spotted it the night before.

They soon knew why it hadn't been seen! It wasn't there. They stared about, puzzled and bewildered. Where could the boat be?

'Did anyone tie it up?' asked Pat, trying to remember. 'No, nobody did, we just pulled it up on the sand. The storm must have swept it away. We'll look for it.'

They began a silent, rather depressed search

for the boat. David found it at last and called the others. He pointed sadly into the deep water off the east side of the island.

'There's the boat,' he said. 'Sunk to the bottom, see? You remember it was leaking badly. Well, I suppose the storm took it round here, and it filled and sank.'

Everyone was silent. This wasn't so good. Now, with their boat gone, they had no way of escape. What a dreadful disappointment!

17 Prisoners again!

It really was a terrible blow to find their boat sunk. It was quite impossible for them to raise it up, the water was too deep. Pat gave a sigh.

'Bang go our beautiful plans!' he said at last. 'We've escaped from Brinkin Towers to this island – only to find we're prisoners here, now!'

'I suppose it's too far to swim?' asked David, hopefully.

'Yes,' said Pat. 'Too far for Tessa, anyway. She can't swim very far. Faith can't either, can she?' .

No, Faith couldn't. They stared at one another gloomily.

'This kind of thing always happens when you count your silly chickens,' said David, crossly, scowling at poor Faith. 'I warned you last night.'

'That's got nothing to with it,' said Faith. 'It *did* seem as if things were going right last night, you know it did!'

They decided to have a bathe, even if they did

feel very gloomy. It did them good. After a little
splashing and giggling they all felt much better.
They clambered out, hungry and glowing.

They made an excellent breakfast off some
sardines in a tin, more biscuits, and butter (also
out of a tin), finishing up with pineapple chunks
and some condensed milk.

'Jolly good,' said David. 'I can't think why
people don't always have meals like this. As for
pineapple chunks, I really believe I could go on
eating them all day long – so sweet and squishy
and pineapply.'

'Idiot,' said Faith. 'You're plain greedy, that's
all.'

'Let's have a talk about things,' said Pat, when

they had finished. 'We ought to make some sort of plan. Goodness knows what, though.'

'What do you suppose the fellows up in Brinkin Towers are doing, now they've missed us?' said David. 'Miss Twisley usually came in to wake us about a quarter to eight. It's almost eleven now. We'll have been missed for some hours.'

'They'll wonder how we got out through a locked door,' said David, grinning.

'They'll have searched the house thoroughly, to begin with,' said Pat. 'They're probably still doing that. Then they would search the grounds – and probably find where we got over the wall, and begin to hunt everywhere.'

'Do you suppose they would think we'd come to this island?' asked Tessa, anxiously.

Pat thought for a moment, then he shook his head. 'No, I don't think so. They have probably completely forgotten about that old, ruined boatshed and the mouldering boat.'

'They didn't see it here last night, either, because it had sunk,' said Tessa. 'Unless they thought of us swimming here, I doubt if it would enter their heads, that we might be in the temple – and swimming wouldn't be very likely!'

'You're right. The island is a good way from the mainland,' said David. 'And it would have meant swimming at night. No, they *couldn't* guess we were here. Anyway, I don't think it would occur to them that we were actually in the very place they had planned to imprison us themselves! I think we're pretty safe from discovery here.'

'Who's counting chickens *now*?' demanded Faith. David took no notice of her.

'It looks as if we are in for a fairly long camping holiday!' he went on, with rather a shaky laugh.

'We've plenty of food,' said Pat. 'But it won't last for ever. Anyway, if things get bad, I'll have a shot at swimming to the mainland. I could make my way back home somehow.'

'They'll have found our bikes by now, I expect,' said Tessa, suddenly. 'Blow!'

'*That'll* puzzle them!' said Pat, with a grin. '*Two* bikes! They'll be worried. Who owns the second – and where is he?'

'She, you mean,' said Tessa. 'They'll see mine is a *girl's* bike. Gosh – won't they be mad! They'll wonder wherever *I* am – and maybe guess I had something to do with letting you all out of that locked room.'

'They'd be right,' said Faith, finishing the last of her gingerbeer. 'Well, we may as well enjoy this unexpected camping holiday. But what about your mother, Pat – won't she be worried about you?'

'No – because she's had to go up to London for a while, and she said we could camp out if we

97

wanted to,' said Pat. 'I'm glad. I'd hate her to worry.'

That first day was rather peculiar. Nobody could quite get used to the idea that although they were apparently on holiday, actually they were prisoners on the island. True, nobody knew they were prisoners except themselves – but they were, all the same. Unless someone took them off in a boat, there they would have to stay!

'I keep feeling all happy and carefree and giggly,' said Faith, 'and then I suddenly remember we can't get away, and it depresses me. I go all gloomy.'

'Oh, you'll get used to it after a few weeks,' said David. Faith looked so alarmed at this remark that they all laughed. She gave her brother a thump.

'*You're* counting the wrong *sort* of chickens!' she said. 'I'd love this for a few days – but not for ever! Not even for three weeks.'

'It may come to that,' said Pat, soberly. 'We must be sensible and face up to things. We're in a fix, you know, and I'm not sure that after today we oughtn't to begin to ration out the food a bit!'

What a truly horrible thought! They all fell on poor Pat and pummelled him for his alarming speech – but secretly, of course, they knew he was right. They *were* in a fix!

18 A visitor to the temple

And now began a queer kind of holiday for the four children. They couldn't get away from the little island, but they had plenty of delicious food and drink, and at night, if the weather was warm and fine, which it usually was, they could sleep out of doors wrapped in the rugs.

If it happened to be cloudy and cold they could sleep in the queer little temple. They could paddle and bathe to their heart's content, and race about all day long if they liked. And yet it wasn't like a proper holiday.

'We've always to be on the look-out in case anyone comes,' complained David. 'We've always to be careful not to shout too loudly, or squeal too much for fear we're heard.'

'I know. It spoils things,' said Faith. How long have we been here now? I even lose count of the days.'

Pat hadn't lost count though. He had notched a stick at the end of each day, so that they would know how long they had been there.

He showed them the stick. 'Look – four notches already – and I'm just going to add another. We've been here five days – and I bet my mother is home and getting worried. I wonder if she's notified the police.'

She hadn't. She had written them a letter saying she would be away for nine days, alas, but would be back then without fail. Would they please write to her and tell her if they were managing all right? And was Mrs Hall keeping an eye on them as she had arranged?

They hadn't written back, of course, because they hadn't had her letter!

'Just like Pat and Tessa,' she thought, half-amused and half-annoyed. 'Little monkeys – they do hate letter-writing, I know. Still if anything had gone wrong they would have let me know at once. I expect they are happily camping out as they planned.'

They were certainly camping out – but not quite as they had planned! It seemed rather strange to be so cut off from the world, and from newspapers and the radio.

'Why, someone might have landed on the moon, and we wouldn't know a thing about it!' complained David.

'Good thing too, if we didn't,' said Tessa at once. 'All the same – I'd like to know if

Mummy's back again or not. I'm beginning to miss her.'

The sixth night came – and with it, a queer thing happened. The children were asleep in the temple, and no one heard the sound of quiet footsteps outside. Not until the front door opened and shut did anyone wake up.

Then Pat awoke with a jump. He sat up, scared, and poked the others quickly. They were lying in the same room as before, and there was no time to get up and hide.

'Someone's in the temple,' whispered Pat, in David's ear. David already knew – he had heard quiet, padding footsteps in the passage beyond, but whoever had made them had gone into a smaller room, a room where only three carved figures sat, silent and forbidding.

A muttering sound came from the room, then a low, chanting noise, and then a kind of wailing song. It really scared the listening children.

'Who is it? What is he doing?' whispered Faith. 'I simply daren't get up to see.'

Pat was the only one who dared to move out of his rug. He slipped it aside and without a single sound rose to his bare feet. He tiptoed across the floor to the door and stood there.

A light shone in the little room beyond the passage way. The chanting and muttering came from there. Pat squeezed into the passage, not even daring to open the door a little wider in case it squeaked.

He came to the door of the little room. He peered through the crack.

What a strange sight he saw! A small man was on his knees before the biggest image, knocking his forehead against the floor as he chanted a wailing little song.

He had placed a small, queer-shaped lamp at the feet of the brooding figure, and as the light caught it it seemed almost as if the eyes of the image were alive. They were ruby-red, and glowed like fire.

Then the little dark man rose to his feet, muttering solemnly. Pat craned his neck to see what he was going to do, but it was difficult to make out anything in the dim light. The little man seemed to be touching the forehead of the carved figure.

He suddenly looked round as if he had sensed that Pat was watching. In fear the boy drew back, hoping he had not been seen. He tiptoed to the others, and whispered into David's ear what had been going on.

'I don't think the fellow knows anyone is here,' whispered Pat. 'If we don't make a sound he may go away without looking into this room.'

'Couldn't we go and sit cross-legged behind that group of figures over there?' whispered David. 'Then, if he did come in, he'd see nothing but a mass of images all sitting cross-legged together.'

'Yes – it might be a good idea,' said Pat. 'I'll tell the girls.'

Very silently indeed the four of them rose to their feet, lifted their rugs to one side, and went behind the silent crowd of images, which were all set up as if in a museum.

They sat themselves down cross-legged, and waited there, their hearts beating far too loudly.

'Like pistons,' thought Pat, trying to breathe slowly so that his heart might slow down a little. But, at a noise outside the door, it began to beat twice as quickly – thump – thump, thump-thump, thump-thump!

Someone was looking into the room – someone holding a little, queer-shaped lamp, someone whose clothes were dripping wet! How still the four children sat – as still as the carved figures that surrounded them!

19 The enemy again

The man with the lamp gazed for what seemed a very long time at the crowd of cross-legged figures. Faith thought suddenly that this would be just the moment when one of them wanted to sneeze!

No sooner had she thought that than she felt a little movement from David, beside her. Poor David – to his utter horror he had felt a sneeze coming. He stopped breathing. He pressed his lips tightly together. He did not dare to hold his nose, for that would mean raising his arm.

The sneeze swelled up. He *couldn't* give the others away by sneezing; it would be dreadful. The sneeze came nearer – and then it exploded.

'WHOOOOOOOSH!'

David was famous for his sneezes – but this was a really outsize one, a most magnificent specimen. It not only startled David; it startled the other three children, too.

But it startled the little watching man most of

all! He gave a loud howl and dropped his lamp to the ground, where it promptly went out. He took to his heels and fled down the passage to the front door, still howling in utter panic.

The door slammed and the children heard running footsteps, and then the sound of a tremendous splash as the little fellow dived into the lake.

Pat almost fell off the table he was sitting on, he was laughing so much.

'Oh David,' he gasped, 'what a sneeze! I almost ran for the door, too!'

Faith and Tessa howled with laughter and relief. Tessa mopped her streaming eyes.

'You made me jump out of my skin, David,' she said, half crying and half laughing. 'Did you do it on purpose? You scared that little fellow into the middle of next week!'

David grinned feebly. He had given himself a terrible shock, for he had honestly thought that a sneeze would give the whole show away. But it hadn't. It had simply scared the man off at once.

'He must have thought one of these images had caught a cold or something,' he said, and began to laugh thankfully. 'I tried to keep the sneeze back – but it only made it all the bigger when it did come.'

'Good thing too,' said Pat. 'You certainly scared off the enemy. I wonder what he came for

– he looked to me as if he was praying to that image in the other room. He must have swum across – he was soaking wet! Do you suppose it's safe to go to sleep again?'

David thought it was, but it was some time before everyone dozed off. Faith kept breaking out into giggles and that made everyone wide awake again.

In the morning they went into the other room to see if the little man had left anything there – perhaps some food. But he hadn't, of course, and, as Pat sensibly said, why *should* he leave food? Images didn't need to eat, and obviously their enemies had no idea the four children were there. All the man had left were small pools of lake water on the floor.

They looked at the three figures in the little room. They were more finely carved than the others in the temple, and more richly dressed. One image had emerald green eyes, one had sapphire blue eyes, and the biggest one had ruby-red eyes.

'I don't suppose all their jewels and rings and their eyes, too, are *real* precious stones, are they?' asked Tessa. 'I mean– I expect they would be if they were in real temples in their own land – but these are only for show, aren't they? Sort of museum figures?'

'Oh yes – none of these jewels can possibly be real,' said Pat. 'Why, these figures would be

worth thousands of pounds if their jewels were real. Look at this one's eyes – if those emeralds were real, they would be worth a king's fortune.'

Faith was looking at the biggest image, the one with ruby-red eyes. 'Would our Strange Ruby be as big as these red stones in this image's eyes?' she asked. 'What odd eyes he has, hasn't he? They don't match. One stone is bigger than the other.'

'Oh come along – don't let's start staring at these cross-legged fellows,' said Pat. 'They give me the creeps. I'm always expecting them to uncross their legs one night and get up and walk over to us, when we are lying asleep.'

'What a *horrible* thought,' said Tessa, alarmed. 'Why ever did you tell us that? Now I shan't dare to go to sleep at night.'

Pat laughed. 'Nothing would stop *you* from going to sleep,' he said. 'Anyway, it's only my joke. Now – who's for a swim – and then what about opening a tin of sliced peaches?'

It was on the afternoon of that day that something else happened. They were all snoozing in the sun, after a very good meal (all out of tins, of course), when David awoke with a big jump. Surely he had heard something?

He certainly had. A boat was coming swiftly to the island – a boat with four men in it – the three dark-skinned foreigners, including the one with the turban, and also the dour-faced Englishman. All looked fierce and angry.

'He *must* be here,' the Englishman said. 'He could swim like a fish. He swam all the way over – and he's here still. I'm sure! The rat – double-crossing us like that!'

'David – there's no time to do anything!' whispered Pat. 'Creep behind those bushes, quick.'

They slid behind some thick bushes and lay there, as still as mice. The men had not come back to look for *them* – they must be after that strange little fellow who had come muttering and chanting the night before, his clothes dripping wet.

The four men pulled up their boat and went swiftly to the temple.

'David,' whispered Pat. 'I think we'll have time to shin up that enormous tree. We'd be much safer hidden up there; come on.'

The four children had never climbed a tree so quickly in their lives. They peered down from the safety of its branches. Were the men going to search the island?

20 A wonderful idea

'They won't find the little man they're looking for,' whispered Pat. 'He was so frightened at David's sneeze that he leapt into the lake and swam off at once. We heard him!'

'It isn't likely they'll look for us if they're looking for him, then,' said David, thankfully.

'I don't know – they'll find the opened tins and the scattered rugs and things,' said Pat, soberly. 'They'll feel a bit puzzled, to say the least of it.'

The men came out of the temple after a time.

'He's not there,' said the Englishman in disgust. 'Maybe he's hiding somewhere on the island, then. Separate out and work your way round and inwards.'

The island was not very big, and it did not take long to go all round and over it. The men came back to where they had started from, looking angry and puzzled. They actually came to stand under the very tree where the children were hiding!

'He must have been here plenty of times,' said one man. 'He's eaten out of those tins, obviously. The double-crossing toad!'

They discussed the matter both in English and in a foreign language. They slipped from one to another language in a bewildering way, so that the children could not follow half that was said. They moved off at last – and then they stopped once more.

'We'll go round the place once again,' said one of the men. 'I've a feeling there's *someone* here – and if it's Rinji we'll get him!'

Pat parted the leaves anxiously to see where the men were going. They were apparently setting off to the other side of the island. He turned his face to David, and it was so excited and such a brilliant red that David was astonished.

'What's the matter?' he asked in a whisper.

'David – we've a wonderful chance to escape. We'll shin down quickly and rush for the boat – the men's boat,' whispered Pat. 'Tell the girls – and then follow me quick! Hurry!'

What an idea! What a truly wonderful, marvellous idea! In a trice all four children had shinned down the tree, Tessa grazing the skin off one leg, but not even noticing the pain – and were making for the boat that was drawn up in the cove.

A shout suddenly sounded on the air.

'Hey! Look, there are the kids! Well, of all

the— Hey, stop, you kids! Look at them, they've
got the boat!'

The four men were racing towards the children. Tessa, Faith and David were already in the
boat and Pat shoved it off on to the water.

This boat had oars, and he and David each
snatched one. The boat glided smoothly away.

The four men had now reached the cove. They
were shouting all kinds of things in what sounded
like half a dozen different languages, and two of

them were shaking their fists so fiercely that they seemed almost comic. One stooped down and picked up a large stone.

He sent it skimming through the air. It struck the side of the boat with a bang and made the girls jump.

'Lie down in the boat, you girls,' commanded Pat. 'Pull harder, David – we must get out of range. The brutes!'

Another stone hit the boat, and a third fell into the water nearby. A fourth one hit David's oar and made him jump.

'Row harder!' urged Pat fiercely. 'One of us will be hit!'

At last, after what seemed an hour or two, but was really only a few minutes, they were out of range of the stones. The boys did not relax, though – they rowed as if their lives depended on it, and it was only when David fell across his oar with exhaustion that Pat called a halt.

The girls sat up, looking very scared.

'We're safe now,' said Pat, out of breath. 'Gosh, it was a near thing, though.'

'Anyway, we've escaped,' said Tessa, thankfully. Her face suddenly brightened and she looked at Pat with shining eyes.

'Pat! *Pat!* Who are prisoners *now* on that island? The four men! They've no boat – and unless they are jolly fine swimmers, they can't get back to the mainland.'

Everyone began to laugh out of sheer relief. It was wonderful to think that the men were now going to have a taste of being prisoners on that island!

Pat began to row again.

'Take your oar, David,' he said. 'Or you, Tessa, take it. We must make for the mainland at once and telephone the police. They can capture those four men as easy as winking now – and all the others in Brinkin Towers, too, because not one of them will have been warned that the other four are prisoners on the island!'

'Gosh – what a scoop!' said David, pulling at his oar, with Tessa helping him. 'It was a real brainwave of yours, Pat, getting this boat!'

It seemed a long way to the mainland, because they deliberately made for the end farthest from the island in case any of the Brinkin Towers men were along the banks somewhere near. They landed at last, pulling the boat up into the bank where the water was shallow.

'Now to make our way through these thick woods,' said Pat, leading the way. 'And all I hope is we don't lose ourselves – and that we come out somewhere sensible!'

'Yes – where there's a telephone,' agreed David, forcing back a whole mass of brambles. 'What a jungle this is! Did you ever see anything like it?'

21 Handing out the news

The woods they had to wade through seemed more like jungle than ever after half an hour's slow going. And then Pat suddenly spied a path!

'Here's a path!' he shouted. 'Only a tiny one – but a path that people have used. Come on – we'll go more quickly now.'

The woods grew less thick after that and although the path wasn't much of a path, still it helped as a 'guide to somewhere', as Tessa said.

They came out at last into a tiny lane, and walked down it, dirty, torn, and bleeding from a hundred scratches. Not a cottage was in sight.

'We may be miles and miles from anywhere,' groaned Pat. 'This is awful – like a nightmare.'

The lane then turned into a rutted road that ran along between hedges so high that the children couldn't see over the tops of them. Then Tessa pointed out something that cheered their hearts.

'Telegraph poles,' she said. 'Look – over there.'

They made for the telegraph poles and came out on a road – not a main road but certainly a road – which, after the overgrown paths and narrow hedged lanes they had been following, seemed a wonderful sight to them.

And then they saw a farm-cart with a youth driving the clip-clopping horse, looking half-asleep in the hot August sunshine.

The children hailed him.

'Hey! Can we have a lift? Where's the nearest telephone?'

The youth looked at them in surprise and disgust.

'You clear off, you gypsies!' he said, and slashed at them with his whip. The tip of it hit his horse, and the startled animal cantered suddenly down the road, almost upsetting the surly youth from his seat.

'Blow,' said Pat. 'I suppose we do look rather awful. Come on – we'll follow the telephone wires – they must lead to somewhere!'

The very next person they met was a country policeman, cycling slowly along, looking extremely hot. He eyed the children suspiciously as he came near.

'Constable!' called Pat, in excitement. 'Can we speak to you? We've some news.'

The policeman thought that Pat's voice didn't

quite match his unspeakably dirty and torn clothes. He jumped off his bicycle, looking suddenly interested. He had a big red face, a large moustache, and twinkling eyes.

'Got news, have you?' he said. 'What kind of news, now, would it be?'

But before they could answer, he had pitched his bicycle against the hedge and had caught Faith and David suddenly by the arms. They looked at him, alarmed.

'You the Gathergood kids?' asked the policeman, in a voice trembling with excitement. 'Redheads both of you and like as peas! Is your name Gathergood?'

'Yes,' said David, in wonder, trying to wriggle away. 'How did you know?'

The policeman let go David's arm and took a rolled-up newspaper from his inside pocket. He flipped it open – and there, on the front page, to the children's intense surprise, was a photograph of David and Faith.

Underneath there was a long paragraph. It began:

MISSING TWINS

Faith and David Gathergood have been missing for some days now, and are feared to have been kidnapped. They have striking red hair, and can be recognised easily . . .

'See?' said the policeman, triumphantly. 'I always carry pictures of missing folk about with me, just in case, you know – but you're the first I've ever spotted. You come straight along with me now. We'll go to headquarters in Wareton. I'll thumb a lift.'

This was all very sudden and exciting. It was also a great relief to have a competent and sensible grown-up in charge of affairs again. However nice it was to be on their own, there always came a time when grown-ups were much the best people to take charge of things!

A lift was duly thumbed. A surprised and very curious lorry-driver took in five unexpected passengers and a bicycle. The policeman would not give him any explanation, much to his annoyance.

'Ho, you needn't make such a mystery about the kids,' said the aggravated lorry-driver at last. 'You've caught them stealing fruit, the little ragamuffins, haven't you?'

'He has *not*,' protested Faith, indignantly. The lorry-driver winked to himself and enlivened the rest of the journey by inventing out loud all kinds of escapades for which the policeman had arrested them. He certainly had a wonderful imagination, and the children listened, most impressed.

Wareton at last – and the police station. And then the pouring out of a story that interested their policeman and two others very much indeed.

One was an Inspector, a grave-faced, keen-eyed man, who hardly interrupted at all.

Out it all came – Miss Twisley, the false governess, Brinkin Towers, the locking-up of David and Faith – then the coming of Pat and Tessa, and the escape to the island. The sinking of the boat, and the long days of waiting. The visit of the strange little man at night, and the hunt for him next day by the four men – and finally their own escape in the boat belonging to the enemy!

When Pat came to this bit the Inspector suddenly sat up very straight. He reached for a telephone as he shot out a sharp question.

'Those men are still there – on the island, did you say? My word – it's incredible! We must get going quickly on this!'

22 It's all over!

The four children were taken to the wife of the policeman who had brought them in, and she let them have a bath and a brush-up.

'Your clothes!' she said. 'What *will* your mothers say to you?'

Her husband popped his head round the door. He looked extremely pleased with himself.

'Inspector says – can you give these kids a meal?' he said. 'Things are humming! My word, this is a day!'

It certainly was. While the children were eating a fine meal provided by the policeman's plump, cheerful wife, unpleasant things were happening over at Brinkin Towers.

Police appeared at the great gates, and surrounded the grounds. As no one opened the gates, they were forced. Then, warily and cautiously the police moved in on the house.

There were five people there, including the old cook. All were servants or secretaries, and were frightened out of their lives. They protested that they had no idea where their chiefs were.

'Don't worry. We know all right,' said the Inspector, grimly. 'In fact, you'd be surprised at what we know. Search the place, boys. We want that ruby!'

That was another thing the children had learnt with much surprise – the Strange Ruby had been stolen. They put together the bits they heard, and the bits they knew, and decided that the enemy had told the little fellow called Rinji to steal the ruby – and he had done so.

'But instead of going back to them with it, he kept it himself,' said Pat. 'And so they came after him. He may have been going to hide in the temple, if we hadn't scared him off with David's sneeze!'

'I shouldn't mind if the ruby was never found,' said Faith. 'Who wants a thing like that? We don't! We don't even want our great-aunt's money. We want to earn our own.'

'Well, you can always give your money away,' said Tessa. 'That would be lovely. You could give it to poor old people, and children with no parents, and—'

'We'd never be allowed to,' said Faith, gloomily.

'I wonder if they captured those fellows on the island?' said Pat. He didn't have to wonder long, for soon the news came through that all four men had been found hiding in the temple, and had given themselves up with hardly a struggle.

'And now they'll have to explain why they kidnapped two nice red-heads like you,' said the red-faced policeman, beaming at the twins. 'In fact, they'll have to answer a whole lot of awkward questions – including one they say they *can't* answer – and that's where they've hidden the Strange Ruby.'

'They don't know that,' said Pat. 'It was hidden by Rinji, the little foreign fellow who came to the temple the night before we left. *He* knows where it is.'

'We haven't found him, worse luck,' said the big policeman. 'He's out of the country already, likely enough. We'll never know where that ruby is, I reckon.'

There was a silence. Then Pat said something so remarkable that everyone stared in amazement.

'Well – *I* know where it is,' he said.

'You don't!' cried the others, amazed.

'I do,' said Pat. 'I bet you anything I do!'

'*Where?*' demanded Faith.

'Do you remember the biggest image in that little room where the fellow was wailing and chanting last night?' said Pat. 'Do you remember it had eyes of red stones – and we saw that they didn't match? Well – I'm sure one of those eyes was the Strange Ruby – hidden there by the frightened little man! He took out the eye that was there and put your ruby in instead! That's why the eyes didn't match.'

There was a pause as everyone digested this astonishing idea. Then Faith clapped Pat on the back.

'You're right! I'm sure you're right!' she said. 'It *was* the ruby! And I guess it was the one in the figure's right eye, too – I thought it was surprisingly lovely.'

'Well, I'll be jiggered,' said the policeman, in a voice hoarse with excitement. 'Excuse me – I must go and tell the Inspector over the phone. He'll send someone across to the island again, to see if you're right. Well, I'll be jiggered, this beats all!'

Pat was quite right, of course. The Strange Ruby was found pressed into the right eye of the biggest image, just as the boy had guessed. It was brought back that night, and for the first time David and Faith saw their great treasure.

It lay in a box of cotton-wool, a deep red ruby with a strange glowing heart. The four children gazed at it.

'You're beautiful,' said Faith, at last. 'But you're very strange, too. Don't bring bad luck to us, please, because when we grow up, we're going to sell you, and use the money to do some good and worthwhile things. Do you hear me, Strange Ruby?'

The ruby glowed like fire. Pat laughed. 'It's done one good thing already,' he said. 'It's given us all a grand adventure.'

'Yes – and what's more, it's giving us a wonderful holiday with *you*!' said David. 'There are four more weeks till we go back to school – and we're going to spend them with *you*! Good old ruby!'

'Looked at it enough?' said the Inspector, coming into the room. 'Well, it's going off to the bank now, and if it's ever stolen again, I'll have to ask for your help, Pat.'

'You shall have it!' said Pat, watching the ruby being wrapped up very carefully. 'My word – these last days have been as good as a book!'

'What would you call the story?' said Tessa. And they all answered at once, in a shout.

'Why – The Adventure of the Strange Ruby, of course!'

BEAVER BESTSELLERS

You'll find books for everyone to enjoy from Beaver's bestselling range—there are hilarious joke books, gripping reads, wonderful stories, exciting poems and fun activity books. They are available in bookshops or they can be ordered directly from us. Just complete the form below and send the right amount of money and the books will be sent to you at home.

☐	THE ADVENTURES OF KING ROLLO	David McKee	£2.50
☐	MR PINK-WHISTLE STORIES	Enid Blyton	£1.95
☐	THE MAGIC FARAWAY TREE	Enid Blyton	£1.95
☐	REDWALL	Brian Jacques	£2.95
☐	STRANGERS IN THE HOUSE	Joan Lingard	£1.95
☐	THE RAM OF SWEETRIVER	Colin Dann	£1.99
☐	BAD BOYES	Jim and Duncan Eldridge	£1.95
☐	MY NAME, MY POEM	Jennifer and Graeme Curry	£1.95
☐	THE VAMPIRE JOKE BOOK	Peter Eldin	£1.50
☐	THE ELEPHANT JOKE BOOK	Katie Wales	£1.50
☐	THE REVENGE OF THE BRAIN SHARPENERS	Philip Curtis	£1.50
☐	FENELLA FANG	Ritchie Perry	£1.95
☐	SOMETHING NEW FOR A BEAR TO DO	Shirley Isherwood	£1.95
☐	THE CRIMSON CRESCENT	Hazel Townson	£1.50
☐	CRAZY SEWING	Juliet Bawden	£2.25

If you would like to order books, please send this form, and the money due to:
ARROW BOOKS, BOOKSERVICE BY POST, PO BOX 29, DOUGLAS, ISLE OF MAN, BRITISH ISLES. Please enclose a cheque or postal order made out to Arrow Books Ltd for the amount due including 30p per book for postage and packing both for orders within the UK and for overseas orders.

NAME . . . .

ADDRESS . . . .

. . . .

Please print clearly.